For Rory

Please play with my poems.

Serious Nonsense
for terribly grown-up people

Ba Mayhew

Published in Great Britain in 2023
by Big White Shed, Morecambe, UK
www.bigwhiteshed.co.uk
Printed and bound by Imprint Digital, Devon

ISBN 978-1-915021-15-1
Copyright © Ben Macpherson
Cover Design & Illustration by Raphael Achache

A CIP catalogue record of this book is available from the
British Library.

For S.C.
who put me on the path to writing

Foreword

Poetry is a beautiful thing: it is pretty, precise, picturesque and powerful. It can be passionate, painful, poignant and pointless. It can be any number of other words that start with the letter 'P', but the thing I enjoy most in poetry is playfulness. As a poet I have the privilege of positioning phrases into patterns and passages. I get to weave words into a mixture of nonsense and stories for you, the person holding this book right now, to enjoy. I am very grateful for that. These poems have been written to be performed and I hope you give voice to them. Find the fun in every verse. There might be rhymes that don't make sense unless you say the words differently. You might need to do silly voices for special characters. You might disagree with the ideas in the poems, in which case; write a new poem that says what you think. A lot of people believe that poetry is scary or hard to understand, others believe that it must be very serious, all about sadness or anger. This is not that sort of poetry book.

Please play with my poems.

Ben Macpherson

Contents

Don't Patronise Children

Don't patronise children.
For children are clever,
Forgetting things never,
Remember forever.
So say it together,
Don't patronise children.

Don't patronise children.
They might know a bit less
But will give it their best.
Whereas adults get stressed,
Well, the kids take a guess.
Don't patronise children.

Don't patronise children.
Just because they are young,
There are songs they've not sung.
So please count me among
All the kids having fun.
Don't patronise Children.

Don't patronise children.
For they've young minds to hone
And they learn as they're shown ,
Plus they choose, once they've grown,
Your retirement home.
Don't patronise children.

Joshua Waite
who Slouched and was Eaten by a Fish

Can you recall Joshua Waite?
Who'd never ever stand up straight.
He was a boy, like boys you know
But always kept his shoulders low.
If running round or on the couch,
Young Joshua would always slouch.
One day mum said, "it's about time
To have a doctor check his spine."

To find out the malefactor,
They met with a chiropractor.
This doctor knew a special trick
To make Joshua's spine go click.
She tried her best, (she went chartreuse)
But what she did was little use,
For even though he went crack! crack!
Josh always chose to bend right back.

Mum, who had felt lost, felt lost-er,
Worrying about his posture
And each day as Josh's shoulder slumps,
Mama would feel down in the dumps.
One day after his deepest slouch,
Joshua started crying ouch!

He tried his best to stand up straight
But simply could not elevate,

As turn by turn his vertebrae
Abandoned him and went away
And one by one his many bones,
Each vanished from their normal homes.

After 10 minutes maybe more,
Joshua flopped down on the floor
And seeing him you could not guess,
The boy was now this squiggling mess.
But mother knew, as mothers do,
Together she put two and two.
Through tears cried "bless his cotton socks."
And scooped him up into a box
She sadly said, "what are the odds?"
And stored him by dad's fishing rods.

Then needing a pick me upper,
Nipped off for a cake and cuppa.
Upon returning from her scone
She found that Joshua had gone.
Mum could not see how she'd missed him,
Lacking his skeletal system.
She searched the house, she'd made a tip,
Dad came back from his fishing trip.

And hurriedly mum then explained,
As Dad's expression grew quite pained.
Said father, who was red of face:
"I've used our son to catch a plaice.
For when I saw inside the tub,
I thought it was a massive grub."

So stand up tall, lest you may turn
Into a spineless wriggling worm.
That's what befell Joshua Waite
Who ended up as fishing bait.

A Biography of the Poet through Language

Once born it comes as no surprise,
I used to only speak in cries
And after passing several weeks,
I got quite good at using shrieks .
It then became my fondest wish
To only speak in gibberish.
I tried to copy every sound
And though the meaning was profound,
Few people really got to grips
With what I meant by gurgled blips.
I gradually was learning words
Like digger, car and trees and birds
And then before the age of two,
A metaphor made its debut.
A small flash of the poet shows,
Insisting eyes were called windows.

Upon reaching the age of four,
It's off to school to learn much more;
Like how to spell and write in lines,
Still things I struggle with sometimes;
Enjoying words I thought were neat,
Like "virtually" said on repeat
And whilst all this is going on,
I'm fleshing out my lexicon.

Analogies and turns of phrase
And clever words fill up my days,

Complicating definition,
Concepts stretched beyond cognition.
I now know words longer by far
Than trees and digger, birds and car.
Words so precise and very niche -
I'm back to talking gibber-iche.
But speaking in my own defence,
There's nothing wrong with some nonsense.

The Creakers

Perhaps one day you noticed,
Whilst climbing up the stair,
When you put your foot down,
It always creaks just there.

People may well tell you,
That this is just the wood,
But I will say the truth,
Like everybody should.

In certain bits of pine,
Cherry, oak, elm or yew,
Live a small ensemble,
And singing's what they do.

They do not know the words,
They sadly missed their turn.
By not attending school,
They never got to learn.

So instead of lyrics,
The group just sings a sound,
To let each other know
When big folks are around.

Should you put your foot down,
And should the step go creak,
Then you must be careful,
And listen when they speak.

If at night you're woken,
Then do not be afraid.
You might hear them creaking,
Their midnight serenade.

Omar Peterson
who Would Never Keep his Mouth Closed

Omar Peterson was inclined
To speak whatever filled his mind.
A foible which might have been quaint,
Had Omar ever shown restraint
But alas thoughts good and bad,
Were shared on impulse by this lad.
And grown-ups thought it rather bold,
To be told by a twelve year old,
About the many kinds of faults,
That they'd acquired as adults.

To set the scene, a summer's day
And whilst the others were at play
Omar, separate from his peers,
Reduced the local mayor to tears
By sharing thoughts about the town.
It really brought the poor man down.
When someone cried "look over there!
A beast is in the market square!"
Before somebody intervened,
A house was promptly smithereened.

It's possible you've not, before,
Laid eyes upon a manticore
So if you are among this tribe,
Permit me whilst I now describe,

A lion's body, lean and tan,
The keen alert head of a man
And if this doesn't make you wail;
From its rump a scorpion's tail
Was arched up high ready to fight.
No wonder it inspired fright.

Bystanders ran, whoosh they were gone,
Except for Omar Peterson.
Opinions bubbled in his brain
And so he started to exclaim,
"You're ugly - your tail's far too long
Your claws look sharp - your jaws look strong
Your eyes are wild - your fur's a mess."
All this and more he did confess
And when at last his rant ended,
Manticore was quite offended.

It reared up high, let out a roar
And did what no one'd done before.
As the timid boy stood quailing,
This beast listed every failing.
"For one so young, you're very loud,"
The monster said, "and far too proud.
So who are you to criticise,
My messy fur and wild eyes?
Your nose too small, your teeth askew
So much you simply cannot do."

Now desperately Omar sought
To find a fault, for his retort
But Omar's mind was fully blank.
His spirit and opinions sank.
The situation headed south,
He found himself inside its mouth.
Yet before he was chewed to mush
He said "Your teeth could use a brush"
Though he cried this out with ardour,
The manticore just chewed harder.

And then left this ferocious scourge.
When folks began to re-emerge,
No matter who you did consult,
All said that it was Omar's fault.
For it was he, who'd been the cause
of passing through the monster's jaws.
Had he just thought 'bout what he said,
Young Omar would not now be dead.
So keep opinions off your mind,
Unless they're helpful, or they're kind.

Do not Read this Poem

Sue De'Nym was not her name.
What it was I can't explain,
Owing to an edict sent
Straight to me from Parliament.
She was tall, her hands like bricks
She used to work for MI6
And still might do today.
(Sadly I'm not free to say)
She might be a world class spy,
(Possibly that is a lie).

She may well have saved us all,
More times than I can recall;
Rescuing some diplomats,
And royal pets, dogs and cats,
And defused a massive bomb,
Skydived into Vietnam,
Chased through streets in super cars,
Stopped someone from stealing mars.
If you read between the lines,
She saved the world many times,
And would never take a break.
(Or all of this could be fake).

The reason we can't find fact –
The official secrets act.
Which, when it was enacted
Ordered her work be redacted.

And if you value your health,
I would keep this to yourself
If you don't, you may well meet
Sue De'Nym whilst in the street
But if you do, don't resist.
(That is, if she does exist.)

The Bus Stop

A bus stop in East London,
More specifically Brick Lane,
Managed to uproot itself,
And never stopped again.

It hopped on the number eight,
Which drove all the way to Bow,
The chaos which entailed,
That bus stop could not know.

For all the other buses,
And their drivers, so astute,
Had to meet the Brick Lane stop,
To carry on their route.

So whilst the stop reached Bow Road,
TFL began the search,
To find that missing bus stop,
Wherever that stop lurked.
The bus stop had its own plan,
To see each and every sight,
He started off for Greenwich,
By Docklands Rail, Light.

And whilst the stop was on tour,
There rose up a massive fuss,
From passengers trapped inside,
Each redirected bus.

They caused such a palaver,
The prime minister was called,
They only thing they asked,
Was, "is GPS installed?"

The stop, had in the meantime,
Been to Soho and Chelsea,
To watch things in theatres,
And carouse the wealthy.
Now London was in crisis,
The buses had all stopped,
The roads were all in gridlock,
But on the bus stop hopped.

The chief of transport police,
Replied, when asked the question,
"What happens when you catch it?"
"Charge it with congestion."

Now, if it were you or me,
We'd feel terrible I know,
But by now the bus stop reached
An airport called Heathrow.

He checked in at the front desk,
Got on a flight to Spain.
That bus stop is still travelling,
And never stopped again.

Headmasters and Headmistresses

Headmasters and headmistresses,
Those whose primary business is
To make the most out of our schools,
To set out and uphold the rules
And make sure kids do what they're told,
Can come in one of seven moulds.

The first is best defined as stern,
Determined that the child will learn.
And if there's trouble they'll exclaim
The offending pupil's family name!
Though they know that times are changing,
Misses still the days of caning.

The second type of principle
Thinks that their school's invincible,
firmly believes that lessons ought
To be cancelled in place of sport.
Wherever they happen to go,
They're covered in the school logo.

The third variety of head
Is often paralysed with dread.
They wonder what they did to deserve
The daily toll put on their nerves.
Chief among their many fears,
A coup led by the lower years.

Type four's the opposite of three,
(And quite the worst, if you ask me.)
It looks like they're working hard, though
Truth be told it's all bravado
And they may seem to know it all,
But what they add is truly small.

The fifth group leads straight from the heart,
And praises music, drama, art.
Their interest, particularly,
Lies extracurricularly.
And if the chance should come to hand
They'd pack it in and start a band.

Type six calls themselves director,
moonlights as a school inspector,
Plays parents off with politics
And knows a hundred PR tricks.
In just a year or two they'll leave
To go somewhere with more prestige.

The seventh one takes bits of each
And misses when they used to teach,
Respects the students and the school
They think that sports and arts are cool
And if you're good and you say please
You might end up with one of these.

Now you know the many features
To sort out all your headteachers
So when you next meet Sir or Miss,

I hope that you remember this,
But don't tell *them* you've worked them out.
They don't want that to get about.

The Time of your Life

I used to think in youthful days
Of everything I'd do,
And with a child's eternity
Achievements I'd accrue.

When a minute felt like hours,
Daily my mind wandered
And every single moment was
Excellently squandered.

Until I started counting time,
Each clock proclaimed the cost,
Of the debt I'd never pay back
The seconds that I'd lost.

I tried to keep things moving fast,
Get more done in a day.
The more efficient I became,
The more time slipped away.

But now my childhood's left behind,
And I must face the facts.
I would have had more time there, if
I'd slowed down to relax.

Arabella
who Could not Stay Within the Lines

As a young girl, Arabella
Loved the colours blue and yella,
Plus red and orange, purple, green
And every single hue and sheen
Of every shade that she could spot,
And trust me that was quite a lot.

Her father wanting to support,
Bought her supplies of every sort;
Oils and pastels, crayons too
And many tubes of glitter glue.
But this was just the very start,
Of his dear girl's pursuit of art.

It happened Sunday afternoon
And Arabella in her room,
Getting fed up of all her chores,
Desired to colour in the doors
With felt tip pens and poster paint
And illustrations rather quaint.

But once her bedroom door was done,
She started on another one!
And when each door from hinge to knob
Was painted, then she changed her job,
And following the muse's call
Turned her attention to the wall.

Her father was about to shout
When Arabella's paint ran out.
But then to her papa's dismay
She used collage and macrame.
Then, for she was versed in culture,
Bedecked the garden path with sculpture.

So much did she pursue this oeuvre,
She turned her house in to the Louvre
And father really quite beside
Himself, then turned and lamely tried
Some control, alas belated.
All had been Redecorated.

There is an upside to this tale.
As when the house went up for sale;
For all the art within its grounds,
It sold for near six million pounds.
That was just a lucky caper.
If you do art, stick to paper.

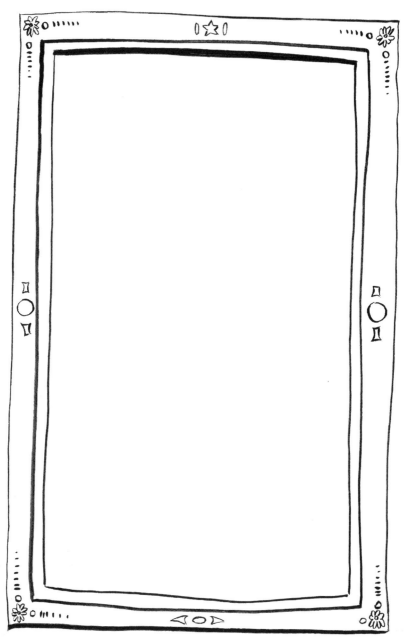

Grab some crayons and have a doodle!

The Beetle in my Brain

There is a beetle in my head,
Who whispers horrid things to me
And I try hard to ignore him,
Despite his tenacity.

He tells me that my friends are false.
I'm nothing but a waste of space.
The things I do are terrible.
I can only bring disgrace.

This beetle got into my brain,
One night when I was tucked in bed.
He mutters words which sadden me
When they echo round my head.

Now, it's true sometimes I listen
And I get shaken up inside
Until I talk with those I love
Who become insecticide.

And I hope you never get one,
A talking beetle, like I do
But remember if he does speak,
Nothing that he says is true.

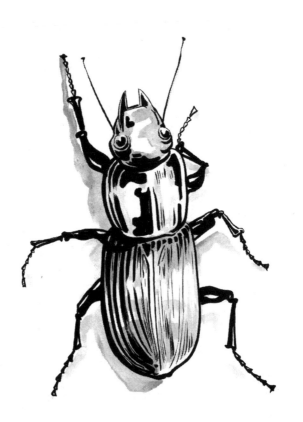

Elizabetta Harker-Wise
and the Lessons we can Learn from History

Elizabetta Harker-wise
Would never ever modernise.
She liked the way things had been done
And loudly told to everyone,
That her opinion of the truth
Was things were better in her youth.
The good old days, she used to say,
Were much more simple than today.

If you offered a computer,
You'd have thought you'd tried to shoot her.
A time she'd have thought's terrific
Best described as neolithic,
Before we'd started smelting bronze
And totting up our many wrongs.
Before our tools made us rueful,
Troubles then were sabre-toothful.

One day, as the sun was dawning,
Floods arose with little warning.
The people seized whatever floats
Like fences, doors and motorboats.
The current carried off this fleet
And drew in more from every street
Until at last this sorry lot,
Were picked up by a mega-yacht.

That is to say except for one,
Who knew how things used to be done
And knowing what she ought to do,
Carved out, by hand, a large canoe
And if you saw the waters rise,
You would have seen Miss Harker-Wise
Paddling, with undue pride,
In her canoe against the tide.

Washed out to sea both boats turned back
And started on the homeward tack.
The yacht sailed on with certain ease,
The motors working with the breeze.
They asked Elizabet aboard
But all she said was 'No, dear Lord.'
And to prove she'd need no backing,
In their wake began kayaking.

But turning round, each face dismayed,
The woman stuck in retrograde
Was nowhere for their eyes to find.
Alas! She had been left behind.
So recall Elizabetta
And make sure you don't regret a
Wat'ry fate amid the kelp,
Because you'd not use modern help.

The Importance of Travel

Travel, travel and see the world!
Go to places you've never been.
Get lost whilst having adventures
And let me know what you have seen.

You must visit far flung cities
And walk some distant boulevard.
Struggle with other languages,
If understanding them is hard.

Visit each of the tourist sites
And then get off the beaten track!
Do it just like the locals do
And tell me all when you get back.

For the world can seem enormous,
Far too much for woman or man
But you don't have to see it all,
Just as much of it as you can.

My Dad and his Bees

It's such a time to be alive
When father opens up his hive,
To check on bees, you get the gist -
The actions of an apiarist.
So with caution and care to boot,
He gets into his keeping suit
An all in one to do the job'll
Make him seem he's from Chernobyl.
His smoker has been lit and prepped
And down the garden he has crept,
Until behind the shed he sees
The corner where he keeps the bees.
And covered so his skin is hid
He gently raises up the lid,
Making sure to be aware o'
swarms of Apis Mellifera.
The super's stacked atop the brood
And when he looks inside, he coos.
The contents are all gold and runny,
Every cell is filled with honey.
Such produce you have never seen,
From worker bee and drone and queen.
To put it simply, there is lots,
Filling more than Seventy pots.
So there's a tale, told to please,
About my Dad who keeps his bees.

The Water Voles

The water voles beneath the bridge
Meet up most Thursday nights,
To share all that they've learnt that week
And set the world to rights.

With knowledge they've squirrelled away,
Each water vole will speak.
The others listen patiently
And groom each whiskered cheek.

Now some of them will rabbit on
And if they're stopped they bawl.
Whilst some are quiet as a mouse,
And barely speak at all.

If you tell this to most grown-ups,
They might not believe ya,
But every day the voles are working,
Busy as a beaver.

They might run off if you see them,
As though they've had a scare.
But if you think that they're frightened
You're mad as a March hare.

They're running for their pencil case,
So they can make some notes,
To get prepared for Thursday night,

With facts on birds and boats.

So now you know of water voles
And how they love their facts.
Just one more thing to remember,
Don't call them water-rats.

Architects

The most ruthless hunters I ever met,
And throughout my life I have met a few,
All gave their profession as architect;
Their merciless hunts, I'll explain to you.

When you see a building, you maybe have thought
That it is just bricks, cement and some wood
But buildings aren't built, in fact they are caught,
By people who never do anything good.

These awful people will train half their life-
Learn how to use blueprints, rulers, stencils
And innocent buildings suffer their strife,
Architect-caught in paper and pencils.

You one day may think, "That looks majestic"
If you are looking at roofs, walls and beams.
Whether commercial or it's domestic,
Architects caught them with back handed means.

For we ought to let buildings range freely,
And let all pillars stand up on their own.
Let buttresses fly overhead breez'ly,
And we would all live in mobile homes.

And the draughtsmen could all be arrested.
They'd be locked up in prison for their crimes,
And no doubt architects would detest it -
Trapped in a jailhouse that wanders sometimes.

Arthur, who Complained too much and Had a Second Shower

Some folks will never be happy,
A fact I learnt later than most,
At a hotel over breakfast,
As I'd started eating my toast.
There was a visitor staying,
A fellow called Arthur Calldraine,
And since his arrival last night,
All Arthur had done was complain.

The cab had driven the long way,
On his bed the mattress too soft,
When asked if there was a problem,
Then Arthur half-heartedly scoffed.
He'd packed his luggage too heavy,
The shower ran hot then too cold,
The staff did their best to placate,
And made changes when they were told.

I chalked all these things up to travel,
As journeys can mess with your head,
But complaining started again,
As soon as he got out of bed.
He terrorised staff with demands,
Asked for things way, way, beyond reason.
A concierge looked at me weeping,
"He's staying here for the season."

At last he came down to breakfast,
Though his moaning didn't abate,
And though he got what he ordered,
He just groaned and looked at his plate.
When asked by the hotel's waiter,
What on earth had gone wrong this time,
He glumly looked at his water.
'I wanted sliced lemon, not lime.'

The waiter went to replace it,
Setting it down on the table,
He turned then to leave but Arthur,
Caught him before he was able.
There's not enough lemon in there,
Was what Arthur rudely had said,
Quite justified, the waiter sighed,
And emptied the glass on his head.

Arthur was shocked, I was laughing,
For none of his problems were real,
And at this soggy comeuppance,
Turned my focus back to my meal.
And as Arthur sat there sodden,
The thing I learnt from this chappie,
Though you might bend over backwards,
Some folks will never be happy.

The Tragic Death of a Pigeon due To Greed, Blind Faith and Local Predation

A pigeon stood upon a ledge.
It cooed and looked around.
It leapt out forward then flapped it's wings,
And fell down to the ground.
It picked at someone's lunch remains,
Scattered across the lawn,
When a passing cat attacked it
And now it is pige-gone.

The Bazoo

The Bazoo is a bird with four feathers.
It has wings as wide as a bus,
And between them is skin like old leather,
Which they preen with suitable fuss.

The Bazoo has a bill like an old boot.
Its cry is quite hard to define.
It's sort of a screech, it's sort of a hoot,
And hearing it shivers your spine.

Although it's lucky for us, the Bazoo,
Is almost unspeakably rare.
In all of my life, I've just heard of two,
Who roost every night on a chair.

Bazoo's like to eat little old ladies.
They swoop down and snatch from above,
Then they guzzle them down like they're gravy.
It's really the wrinkles they love.

But I've heard of Bazoo's with a hunger,
And I'm not sure if this is true,
For meat that's considerably younger,
So you must beware the Bazoo.

Titania Blake Who Was Popular
and Torn To Shreds

Miss Titania Blake, of great renown,
Was widely sought after about the town
And owing to her popularity
An evening off was quite the rarity.
In every afternoon and morning too,
Titania had things she ought to do.
For when she received an invitation,
She accepted without hesitation,
And paid no attention to day or date,
Which led to the most unfortunate trait -
Not appearing when she was expected,
In spite of offers she had accepted.

People were first upset, and then surprised
To find their invites'd not been diarised
Understandable, when you've invited
An individual so short-sighted.
Now Titania gave many excuses
Although each of them served little use as
She missed events, both causal and formal,
So her absence was considered normal.

The day was sunny, the skies were blue,
Titania's friends had déjà vu.
It was Sunday brunch and whadayaknow,
Titania once again had failed to show.

Now, brunches Titania'd missed plenty
But this time her friend was turning twenty,
And when she found Titania lackin'
'Twas the straw that did the camel's back in.

And by coincidence, at that same point
Other people, with noses out of joint
We're all mysteriously inspired
To band together and start to riot.
Now this mob was hunting for Titania
Who was watching Chekhov's Uncle Vanya.
At the theatre in the matinee,
A decision she had just made that day.

The horde burst in the auditorium,
Lacking all of the due décor-ium!
Then, hoisted up, by her legs hands and feet,
Titania was carried into the street.
Everyone yelling their invitations,
Reminding her of her obligations.
Still carried, Titania felt woozy
And wished then that she had been more choosey.

The birthday party just couldn't believe,
They all seized her arm and started to heave,
But her other friends wouldn't have that at all,
So they clutched a limb and started to haul.
The doctor, the vet, the man from the bank,
Grabbed hold of her leg and started to yank,
And just as it seemed that the mob was flagging,
Many more arrived and started dragging.

Now horrible things like this seem fated,
As each of her limbs were dislocated,
Titania passed out from the ag'ny.
Pop! like a cork straight out of champag'ne.

That night when her friends returned to their beds,
Each of them carried Titania's shreds.
Just making it clear, in case you wonder,
The miserable girl was torn asunder.
The findings from the police enquiry
Ruled cause of death was lack of diary.

So a piece of advice, to you, from me
If you read the letters RSVP,
Remember that your attendance matters,
Or else you too may end up in tatters.

Any Port in a Stilton

"Any port in a Stilton!" The captain roared.
A song he'd learnt by wrote,
Whilst swinging wild his cheese knife,
From atop his gravy boat.
And the crew about him shivered,
How long had they been at sea?
Sailing round the tabletop,
For next to eternity.

"Any port in a Stilton!" their captain's cry,
As the bosuns whistle blew,
Jobs were quickly stowed away,
And stood to alert the crew.
As their captain inspected,
They inspected him the same,
This proud and salty sea dog,
And his ongoing refrain.

"Any port in a Stilton," bellowed his eyes,
And port was stained in his beard.
Blue were his veins like Stilton,
Wherever his skin appeared.
He'd sailed round soups and dishes
Passed plates, since he was a lad,
But when the sea was calm,
The captain would stare off sad.

"Any port in a Stilton!" he would whisper,
His eyes filling up with tears,
At the thought of his belov'd,
Lost to the passage of years.
They'd also sailed the table,
Till one day they sailed no more,
That day the captain had sworn,
Ne'er to return to the shore.

"Any port in a Stilton!" rose the holler,
Whenever adventure called.
And call it did and often,
And the crew followed enthralled.
They met the queen of puddings.
They met the chicken supreme.
They thought their tale was over,
When they all fell in the cream.
Buffeted by the buffet.
marooned upon a meringue.
Washed up on dessert islands
But still the captain sang.

"Any port in a Stilton we find my boys,
Where we can weather the storm!
So let go of the flotsam!
Keep sailing on until dawn!
We have to keep on going,
For our time at sea is short.
Until we find our haven,
In Stilton any a port!"

Boyhood

As a child I was an outlaw.
I ran riot with boys my age,
Our territory 'out of bounds',
The woods beyond a teacher's gaze.
There's architecture among trees,
Vaulted ceilings in a laurel,
A cathedral under willow.
The dens for packs of wild boys.
A self-sufficient break time game.
A currency of sticks and stones,
With potions made of leaves and berries,
And knowledge which children have.

And naturally there was war.

A chaos lacking consequence,
Packs charging down the hill to raid,
Ambushing each other's bases.
A harmless bloodlust once a day.
Mortal wounds walked off by the bell.
Untold juvenile heroics,
Glorious to a nine year old.
Enjoying the savagery of youth.
A world built on collective dreams,
And learn the truth all schoolboys know,
Die bravely, there's maths after lunch.

Farfalle Browning
and a Recipe for Self Ruin

Farfalle Browning, celebrity chef,
Known for her podcast, her blog and her book,
Caused a commotion when she did attest,
Only the gifted should ever try cook.

Now Farfalle Browning, the cooking tycoon,
Whose followers did whatever they're told,
Inspired them all to lay down the spoon
the whisk and the knife, let ovens go cold.

Farfalle Browning, the dinner time snob,
Face of her very own Tupperware range,
And patented way of cleaning the hob,
Looked at her business and thought it was strange.

Farfalle Browning, financially bust,
With all her empire flushed down the pan,
With no one cooking, she'd not earn a crust,
Easy to say it had not gone to plan.

Farfalle Browning had egg on her face,
Stuck with the outcomes of all of her deeds,
So here's some advice, you know, just in case,
When hands are involved, don't bite one that
feeds.

The Tapir

An elephant fell in love with a pig
And the piggy said "Elephant, my dear,
Our love for each other grows everyday,
Let's have a baby and call them tapir."

Both agreed that they would like a baby
And for a while the elephant thunk
"I know they'll be pink with a tail like yours
And as tall as me," she thought, "with my trunk."

What followed, you'll find out when you're older,
But let's say once thirteen months were complete,
If you visited pig and elephant,
You would hear the pitter patter of feet.

But Tapir wasn't tall like elephant,
She was the size of her father the pig.
Her tail didn't curl and her skin was grey,
Even her trunk wasn't really that big.

But the pig and the elephant loved her
She was their baby Tapir after all.
You cannot choose what your children are like,
You love them, whether they're big or they're
small.

Lovely Brie

I like Brie, it's true you see,
For nothing quite compares to Brie.
Mellow taste, soft and creamy,
When it's offered I say, Brie me!
No finer use of curds and whee,
Than making up a lovely Brie.

If ever I visit Paris,
As I have cause occasionally
I will not eat charcuterie,
Nor will I drink a crisp Chablis,
But off to the fromagerie,
And there to buy a lovely Brie.

For if there was a king of cheese,
The dynasty would be the Bries.
As Camembert I cannot bear.
Of Roquefort I can take no more.
At Pont-l'Évêque I scream no heck.
And turn and flee for lovely Brie!

So ask yourself if you were me,
And had to choose the best dairy,
Would you choose butter? Cheddar? Ghee?
Babybel or Dairylea?
The answers really plain to see.
I wish I had a lovely Brie.

Tara Amadeus Wishall Who Lacked Focus and Almost Died as a Result

Tara Amadeus Wishall's
View on life was superficial.
If de-tail was desired,
Tara would not be required.
In short, she was the kind of folk,
Who paints her life with broader stroke.
This habit got her into strife
And very nearly cost her life.
The night about which I'm talking,
Is often used for Guy Fawkeing.
The day had been a mixed melange
Of things going so slightly wrong-ge.
She made a bowl of porridge oats
But threw away the cooking notes.
The microwave tray slowly turned.
She found her porridge fully burned.
Impressive, you'll no doubt exclaim,
As microwaves lack naked flame.

And this was very much the style,
Of things that dogged her all the while.
Things which, if she'd been more precise,
May well have left her day quite nice.
Miss Wishall met up with her friend
And hoping for a better end
To her disaster of a day,
Went to a fireworks display.

To no one but Tara's shock, it
Was required to bring a rocket
But phew, her friend had brought a spare,
Knowing that Tara would be there.

The audience was crowded round
And all gazed skyward from the ground
But Tara did not like her view,
It's hard to see at four foot two.
She took upon the single hope,
To stand beyond the safety rope
And understanding seemed to lack,
Of signs that read "Danger Stand Back"
Before somebody saw this scandal,
Whoosh began a Roman Candle!
At once there was a massive bang,
As upwards many rockets sang.
Now Tara, shocked, started to reel
Beside a spinning Catherine wheel.
And in that pyrotechnics light,
The audience was filled with fright.
As Tara stood in silhouette,
She had an inkling of regret.
The mantra with rockets afire,
Light touch paper then retire,
Ran headlong through the minds of all
And Tara stood in deathly pall.
Her friend, Alice Jane McFrijon,
Being known for her precision,
Leapt forward and pulled her to the floor,
Til not in danger anymore.

The two crawled about on stomachs, prone,
Until they reached the safety zone,
And with awareness Tara wept,
I should have looked before I leapt.

So think before you start to act
And use a modicum of tact.
Keep circumstances well in mind
And never charge in fully blind.
Use your caution, well and of'en,
Or you might not dodge the coffin.

The Thingy

Now I've just had quite a good thought;
The sort of thing you really ought
To write down lest it slips your mind
And you would leave that thought behind.
I know it as a good idea.
It definitely was crystal clear.
Yet as though it has been banished;
It has simply up and vanished.
I know what I had thought before.
What follows, I know even more.
But still the mystery remains.
This thought that has escaped my brains.
The only thing that I'm aware
Of's that the thought's no longer there.
The more I try to get it back,
The harder it becomes to track.
Before too long I will recall
Some thoughts I'd never thought at all
And when I think I've caught this fella,
It flees across my cerebella.
Always it evades detection
Further from my recollection.
Into thoughts so complicated
They are leaving me frustrated
So this idea has fled my head.
Oh I've remembered!

Buy some bread.

Aeroplanes

An aeroplane! An aeroplane!
I surely don't need to explain
The wonder of an aeroplane.
You can fly to Chad, Guam or Spain
And then fly straight back home again,
If you're on board an aeroplane.

An aeroplene! An aeroplene!
Soaring high up, as in a dream,
If you've booked on an aeroplene.
The travel method most supreme,
You'll feel just like a king or queen,
If traveling by aeroplene.

An aeropline! An aeropline!
The engines roar, you start to climb
And take off in the aeropline.
Ascending at a steep incline,
Then levelling off in no time,
When piloting an aeropline.

An aeroplone! An aeroplone!
The envy you'll find, once you've flown
Around the world by aeroplone.
And if the turbulence has blown,
And if around the cabin thrown,
You're safe inside an aeroplone.

An aeroplune! An aeroplune!
You'd think that you could touch the moon,
When flying in an aeroplune.
Over mountain, mesa and dune,
Fly away then come back hume.
The wond'rous thing an aeroplune!

The Wise Man

Once there was a wise man,
Who lived upon a hill,
Which stood by the river -
That river's flowing still.

Word about the wise man,
Travelled throughout the land
And folks would talk about
The thoughts he had to hand.

And it was said of him,
He'd heard a mighty truth,
Wisdom that he'd lived by
Since his earliest youth.

Some people travelled far,
To seek his sage advice,
Trudging up the hillside
And asked ever so nice.

"But my wisdom is clear."
The man said with a frown,
Though people kept coming
And soon they built a town.

The people got fed up,
Impatience I suppose,
Till one night a storm blew
And up the river rose!

The townsfolk fled up hill
And looked back with despair.
The man shared his wisdom,
"The river floods down there."

Don't go seeking wise men,
Instead you can deduce.
Think for yourself and then,
Your house won't be a sluice.

Battenburg Fairy

Somewhere in your home in an overlooked cupboard,
Hides a wee little beastie you've not yet discovered.
In a den in the corner of the uppermost shelf,
The Battenberg Fairy lives all by herself.
The Battenberg Fairy stands six fingers high
And out of her back she has wings like a fly.
She's got short spiky hair, bright eyes as you'd think
And her clothes are alternately yellow and pink.

But she's not some fairy who dances round flowers,
Her nose is all crooked and her face always glowers
Her pale lips are thin and just underneath,
A fine little row of sharp pointed teeth.
At night when all of the house is asleep,
She wakes and gets to her beetle-like feet.
Out of her cupboard she jumps as she titters,
And over the counters she cackles and skitters.
She goes to the fridge and opens the door
And leaps to the third shelf straight from the floor.

She dances on food, right there in the cold
And where her foot touches, starts to grow mould,
Green little spots and white bits all hairy,
That is the spell of the Battenberg Fairy.
She plays with the milk which curdles, all lumpy,
The skins of the peppers wilt and go bumpy
And the trout on a plate, in the exact spot
That she places her foot, the fish starts to rot.

From out of the fridge, to the table jumps down,
She lands on bananas that start to go brown.
And then a madness starts to consume her,
She dances fandango atop a satsuma.
Her tangerine dance floor starts to go blue,
And the fruit in the fruit bowl start to turn too.

She plays with the flies but won't know she's done,
Till her dance is disturbed by the first light of sun.
For at dawn's early light, she beats a retreat
With fast flapping wings and small jumping feet.
Straight back to her shelf to go rest her eyes
She curls up to sleep in a magic disguise.

And if you went looking, I'd forgive your mistake,
For all you would find was a Battenberg cake.

Glossary
(a list of words that might need some explanation)

Abate   Ah-bait
To stop or pause. This explanation will now abate.

Accrue   Ah-crew
To gather or collect. I have accrued words here you
might like to have explained.

Apiarist   Ape-ya-rist
A person who keeps bees but cannot spell
beekeeper.

Apis mellifera   Ay-pis mel-i-ferr-uh
The scientific name for honey bees, in case they
ever become scientists.

Ardour   Ard-er
Enthusiasm or excitement. The 'arder the passion,
the 'arder the ardour.

Asunder   Ah-sun-der
Apart, or into pieces.   Alternatively, sitting atop
your bottom.

Attest   Ah-test
To provide proof for something. Not to be confused
with what you yell at an exam. Argh! Test!

Auditorium   Or-de-tor-ee-um
A place for performing in. Anywhere can be an
auditorium, if you are a big enough show off!

Battenberg Cake   Bat-urn-berg Cake
A cake made of pink and yellow sponge, and
marzipan. Like a chessboard at a fancy dress party.

The Beaten Track   The Bee-tun Track
The usual or popular choice. Also what happens
when you hit a path with a whisk.

Bedecked   Be-decked
To be covered in something, usually nice, or when
you get punched by a bee.

Blueprint   Blue-Print
The plan to show what a building should look like
once it is built. Or a sign you need new ink in the
printer

Boulevard   Bull-eh-vard
A wide road often lined with trees. Not to be a
confused with a bully-vard which is the street that
calls you names as you pass it.

Bravado   Brah-var-doh
Boldness, apparent confidence. Also a way of
describing a really good avocado.

Buttresses   But-ress-es
Supports for walls to make them stronger. Also a
mattress just for your bum.

Carouse   Cah-row-z
To have a noisy party. If you have a noisy party with
horses it's a carousel.

Cerebella   Seh-ruh-be-lah
Parts of the brain that help with movement. For
example Sarah and Bella have cerebella.

Chablis   Sha-Blee
A type of white wine that tastes nice. For example
"This Chablis's not too shabby."

Chartreuse   Shar-troos
A Greeny-yellow colour. The exact shade of
chartreuse may depend on what colour Chart-you-
use.

Chekov   Che-kof
A Russian Playwright. Why was he Russian? 'Cos
his play was late.

Chernobyl   Cher-nob-ill
A site of a nuclear disaster. There really isn't
anything funny about that.

Chiropractor   Kai-roh-prac-tor
Someone who moves back bones around to make
people feel better. Can be located in or outside of
Egypt.

Cognition   Cog-ni-shun
A person's ability to understand. If you understand
clockwork that's your cog-cognition.

Collective   Coh-leck-tiv
A group of individuals or things. You might call a
collective of definitions a glossary.

Comeuppance   Cum-up-ants
A deserved punishment. This glossary was my
comeuppance for writing a poetry book

Commercial   Cum-er-shul
Something that's related to a business. Like you, if
your mum is a bank.

Commotion   Co-moh-shun
A noisy confusion or disturbance. To experience in
real life, get 6-10 friends and start yelling the word
commotion.

Congestion   Con-jest-shun
A blockage or crowding. Or ignoring a prisoner
after a bad joke.

Coup   Coo

A forceful change of power. If there was a riot in a hen house you might call it a coop coup.

Debt   Det

something owed to another person or company. Remember the "B" is silent like a sneaky wasp.

Decorum (Decor-ium)   Dec-or-um

The correct or appropriate way to behave. Tell them of decorum, you know it's gonna bore 'em

Definition   Deh-fi-ni-shun

The meaning of a word. This, for example, is a definition.

Déjà vu   Day-jar voo

The feeling something has already happened.

Déjà vu   Day-jar voo

The feeling something has already happened.

Diarised   Die-er-iezd

To put something in a diary, like an event, not a bookmark.

Domestic   Duh-mess-tik

Something to do with home, as opposed to Dome Stic the world's leading dome repair glue.

Draughtsmen   Drafts-men
People who make detailed drawings. Also people who are really good at playing draughts.

Belated   Beh-lay-ted
Something happening later than planned.

Edict   Ee-dikt
An order, if someone makes too many, they're edict-ed to edicts.

Efficient   Ef-ish-unt
Working well with little waste. Alterntatively the act of hunting fish online.

Enacted   En-ak-tid
To make something into a law. Also what happened when the alphabet put on a play.

Ensemble   On-som-bul
A group of performers. Also the answer to the question "where are the bull horns?"

Entailed   En-tay-uld
The things that follow. My cat's tail entailed my cat

Entrepreneur   On-tru-pru-nur
A person who's job is to make new businesses. A person who doesn't make businesses is an off-trepreneur.

Extracurricular   Ex-tra-cuh-ric-yu-lar
Fun activities outside of the main subjects at
school. Or being very particular about your curry.

Flotsam   Flot-sum
Wreckage from a ship that has floated away. A big
shipwreck means lot-sa flotsam

Foible   Foy-bul
A habit or small weakness. I have a foible for the
word foible, I use it whenever I'm oible.

Gist   Jist
The main meaning of a speech or text. The gist of
this list is the meaning of words

Insecticide   In-sek-ti-side
Something poisonous to bugs. Not to be confused
with insect-inside which is when you swallow a fly.

Lexicon   Leks-ih-con
A collection of words. Like a dictionary but spelled
with fewer letters.

Louvre   Loo-vruh
A palace turned museum in Paris, filled with art.
Also when you hoover the bathroom.

Macrame   Mak-ruh-may
A form of art using threads and knotting. Some
people say it's knot art, others say it is.

Malefactor Mah-luh-fak-tor
The cause of something bad. As opposed to Male
Factor which is the reason something is a boy.

Matinee Mah-tin-ay
A performance in the afternoon. Not to be
confused with a manatee who don't perform at all.

Melange Muh-lonj
A mixture. The spice melange must flow.

Mesa May-suh
A single flat topped hill with steep sides. Keep it
clean, there's nothing worse than a messy mesa.

Modicum Mod-i-cum
A small amount. Sometimes you need a modicum,
sometimes you need a lot-of-em

Muses Mews-es
Goddesses who inspire people to make art. If
what you make is entertaining then it amuses the
muses.

Neolithic Nee-o-lith-ick
Part of the stone age about 6000 years ago. I think
the stone age rocks.

Niche Neesh
A place that is particularly suited to its occupant.
Or a nasty quiche.

Obligation   Ob-li-gay-shun
A task or duty you must do. Like the obligation to
write a glossary for a poetry book.

Oeuvre   Oo-vruh
A collection of work by one creator. The artist
worked on her oeuvre, then she died and it was
over.

Palaver   Puh-lar-vuh
a confusing or complicated action. Unless it is
making a meringue pudding in which case it's a
pavlova.

Patronise   Pat-ron-ise
To talk down to someone. But you already knew
that, didn't you? Because you're so clever.

Plaice   Place
A flat fish found in the sea. If it's not in the sea it's
out of place.

PR   Pee- Ar
Short for Public Relations, how a person or
company talks to the public. Not how you are
related to the public like a second cousin fifteen
times removed.

Preen   Preen
To tidy and arrange feathers. Or a purple sort of
green.

Profession   Pruh-fesh-un
A person's job. If someone catches fish as their job their profession is pro-fishing.

Pyrotechnics   Pie-roh-tek-niks
Fireworks and explosions. Tragically nothing to do with pie at all.

Quailing   Kway-ling
showing fear or nervousness. The quail stood qualing as it's confidence was failing.

Quaint   Kwaynt
Small and cute, often historic. Any sound made by a duck that isn't a quack.

Rarity   Re-ri-tee
Something that is rare or uncommon. Also an unusual cup of tea.

Recollection   Reh-coh-lek-shun
The ability to remember. At least that's what it is if memory serves.

Redacted   Ri-dak-ted
Hiding information on a need to know basis. This has been ████████ .

Renown   Ri-nown
Fame or glory. If you don't want to be famous you should mind your ren-own business.

Retirement   Ri-ty-er-ment
Leaving a job, usually due to old age. The act of
putting new tyres on a car.

Retort   Ree-tort
A reply or response. Alternatively something
referencing German cakes.

Retrograde   Ret-ro-grayd
Something heading backwards. Or coloured in
grey, a long time later.

RSVP   Ar-Ess-Vee-Pee
Short for Respondez S'il Vous Plait, which is French
for please reply in case you want someone to write
back to you in French.

Rueful   Roo-ful
Filled with regret or sorrow. Alternatively, filled
with kangaroos.

Scourge   Skurj
Something that causes pain or suffering. Or the
urge to become Scouse.

Serenade   Se-ruh-nayd
A song for a particular audience. Also a musical
fizzy drink.

Silhouette   Sil-ooh-et

A shadowy outline of a person or object.

Sluice   Sloos
A gate to control the flow of water. More water runs through when the sluice is loose.

Smelting   Smell-ting
A way of extracting a metal. As we all know – Smelt it, dealt it.

Squandered   Skwan-durd
To have wasted something. Alternatively what happened when a squid went for a walk.

Squirrelled   Skwi-rulld
To hide something away for safe keeping, for instance he squirrelled away the squirrel.

Stencil   Sten-cil
A TOOL TO COPY A DESIGN. A TOOL TO COPY A DESIGN. A TOOL TO COPY A DESIGN.

Strife   Stryf
Anger or conflict. A dessert that makes you angry is called a strifle.

Superficial   Soo-per-fish-ul
On the surface. Alternatively a hole in a particularly super fish.

Tack   Tak
Zig zagging into the wind, on a boat. At least it's zig zagging and not spitting.

Tenacity   Tuh-na-si-tee
Keeping on trying again and again. Also a city where everything costs 10 pounds.

Uncle Vanya   Unk-ul Varn-yah
A play written by Chekov. If your mum or dad goes to see it then it's Brother Vanya.

Vertebrae   Ver-ta-bray
The bones that make up your spine. If you stand on your head then they're invertabrae.

Acknowledgements

There are so many people to thank in a book like this and I will inevitably forget someone important, so please forgive me if your name is not here and it should be.

Firstly my family: Mum who first read me poetry, sharing the delightful, and often horrible, rhymes of Roald Dahl, Hilaire Belloc and Spike Milligan. Dad who sets the bar for questionable rhyming in his hilarious, sentimental and lovingly crafted Birthday poetry. My sister Adele, who was the first person I ever wanted to make laugh. There are also grandparents, aunts, uncles, cousins, partners and pets who created a network of support and inspiration.

There are so many friends who I need to thank, especially in the Nottingham poetry and theatre communities. GOBS Collective has been a place to develop, change and challenge my relationship with poetry. Improv has been a place of playfulness and fun. Nottingham Poetry Festival put their faith in me. I especially need to thank Jonny who put up with me living with him whilst I wrote most of this collection and was always an excellent sounding board for whatever bizarre idea popped out of my head next.

I cannot forget Anne & Big White Shed. She is the reason this book physically exists in the first place. Thank you. Similarly, Raph for his beautiful illustrations. Finally, as I knew them then: Miss Crossland, Mr Edwards, Mr Lawrence & Dr Renshaw – all English teachers. You put me on this path. It's all your fault

Bio

Ben Macpherson is a poet, writer and performer originally from Suffolk and currently living in Nottingham. His work has reached people, young and old, and spanned everything from primary school poetry workshops to Arts Council funded plays. His writing has been heard on BBC Radio, through the Nottingham UNESCO City of Literature project, and on stages across the country. Common to all of these works is a sense of playfulness and nowhere is this better shown than in his family focussed poetry. He enjoys stories, myths and legends and loves to cook. He also has quite a lot of Lego.